Gertrude Chandler Warner's

THE BOXCAR CHILDREN GRAPHIC NOVELS

MYSTERY RANCH

Henry, Jessie, Violet, and Benny are spending the summer on their aunt's ranch out west. The ranch is a beautiful place, but Aunt Jane is an unhappy woman who hasn't spoken to their grandfather in years. Can the Boxcar Children help mend things between them? And will an amazing discovery about the ranch change everything?

THE BOXCAR CHILDREN
GRAPHIC NOVELS

THE BOXCAR CHILDREN
SURPRISE ISLAND
THE YELLOW HOUSE MYSTERY
MYSTERY RANCH
MIKE'S MYSTERY
BLUE BAY MYSTERY

Gertrude Chandler Warner's
THE BOXCAR CHILDREN
MYSTERY RANCH

Adapted by Christopher E. Long
Illustrated by Mike Dubisch

Henry Alden

Watch

Jessie Alden

Violet Alden

Benny Alden

Visit us at www.albertwhitman.com.

Adapted by Christopher E. Long
Illustrated by Mike Dubisch
Colored by Wes Hartman
Lettered by Johnny Lowe
Edited by Stephanie Hedlund
Interior layout and design by Kristen Fitzner Denton
Cover art by Mike Dubisch
Book design and packaging by Shannon Eric Denton

Library of Congress Cataloging-in-Publication Data

Long, Christopher E.
  Mystery ranch / adapted by Christopher E. Long ; illustrated by Mike Dubisch.
     p. cm. -- (Gertrude Chandler Warner's boxcar children)
  ISBN 978-1-60270-589-0 [1. Orphans--Fiction. 2. Family--Fiction. 3. Mystery and detective stories.] I. Dubisch, Michael, ill. II. Warner, Gertrude Chandler, 1890-1979. Mystery ranch. III. Title.
  PZ7.W887625Mys 2009
  [E]--dc22
                                    2008036102

Gertrude Chandler Warner's

THE BOXCAR CHILDREN GRAPHIC NOVELS

MYSTERY RANCH

Contents

THE LETTER

A COOL WELCOME

Jessie and Violet were excited to be heading to Aunt Jane's ranch.

The hours passed quickly for the two girls, because everything was new.

At their stop at Centerville early the next morning, the only other passenger got off the train as well.

I'm getting off here, too. May I help you with your bags?

Why yes, thank you.

Thank you for carrying the bags. It was very kind of you.

Not at all.

Are you Miss Alden?

11

Maggie told the children that Aunt Jane rarely ate and that's why she spent all day in bed. But Jessie and Violet were hungry, so they decided to make a wonderful breakfast.

My, that smells good!

Aunt Jane, this is delicious. Violet and I made it for you.

Drink it slowly. As Benny would say, "Don't rush it."

Who's Benny?

Benny is the funniest boy you ever saw, Aunt Jane. He's a great little brother.

And Henry, our older brother, is very clever, kind, and thoughtful.

If your brothers are like you, I'd like to meet them. Now take the glass away. I'm tired.

Jessie and Violet slept well that night. The next morning they were woken by voices. They went downstairs to see who had arrived.

I'm Sam Weeks, your Aunt Jane's neighbor. Nice to meet you. Are you planning to stay here all summer?

We don't really know how long Aunt Jane will want us.

A DAY AT THE RANCH

I'm worried about the two of you. I'm afraid you won't get enough food. Maggie had to eat at our house when she got too hungry.

Well, we can buy food. Grandfather gave us some money.

Maggie and I can take you to the store.

A stranger got off the train last night. I noticed him because not very many people get off that train.

Yes, we know! We call him our mystery man.

During the ride to town, Jessie and Violet made up a telegram to send to Grandfather. They had the station agent send it as soon as they arrived.

Jessie and Violet bought enough food to last a week. Then they returned to the ranch.

When they got back from the store, they found Aunt Jane very cross.

While you were at the store, three men came in here and asked me to sell my ranch. Can you imagine?

I told those three men that my ranch isn't for sale. I've got other plans for it.

THE BOYS COME

In the next couple of days, Aunt Jane started to feel better. She began to eat more as well. Jessie and Violet decided to ask Aunt Jane for a favor.

Aunt Jane, Violet and I miss Henry and Benny.

Couldn't we ask them to come for a few days?

Well, I'd agree to that. But I don't want to see your Grandfather.

Grandfather is really very nice when you get to know him.

Don't forget that I knew your grandfather long before you did. If Henry and Benny turn out like him, back they go!

Tell Benny to bring his dog.

Watch will love the ranch!

THE YELLOW STONES

Now that the children were together, they were very happy. Aunt Jane seemed to be getting more cheerful every day.

One morning, Aunt Jane called all the children to her. She had an important announcement.

I'm going to give you children this ranch. You are the only relatives I have. You seem to be good children, and you have been kind to me.

I know you are not old enough to manage the ranch alone, so I'm gong to bring Sam Weeks into it. He will manage the ranch for you. What do you think about that?

We're too surprised to say much, Aunt Jane! It's wonderful.

I want my ranch to belong to people who love it. That's why I wouldn't sell it to those three men.

The children said "thank you" as they left Aunt Jane to rest.

Aunt Jane had told the children not to get lost. The ranch was very big, so they had to be careful going out on their own.

It's a beautiful place.

We should find a nice cool place to eat our lunch.

The children found a quiet and cool place to eat their lunch.

Look! There's a little hut.

There was nothing in the hut except a fire pit made of stones.

Someone built a fire here, and not too long ago. The stones are still warm. Let's go.

There's no grass here. This field isn't very good.

But it's pretty. See the yellow and black lines in those rocks.

They seem to be made of yellow sand. How strange!

THE MYSTERY MAN

The next day, Aunt Jane had Mr. Pond, who handled her business, come to the house. She wanted to sign the paperwork giving the children her ranch.

Children, this is Mr. Pond.

Hello!

It didn't take long to fill out the paperwork. Aunt Jane wrote her name, and so did Jessie, Henry, and Violet.

Isn't it funny what you can do by just writing your name?

It just gave you children 1,280 acres of land and a big ranch house.

And a hut, too, where someone has been staying.

What? What's that? I didn't know there was a hut on my land.

Sam and I want to see this hut in the woods. Will you take us there?

FAST WORK

Everyone agreed that the only one who could manage the ranch was Grandfather.

I think your grandfather will be glad to help. I can go tell him the whole story.

Aunt Jane didn't want Grandfather coming to her ranch. Maybe she'll be angry if he comes to help.

The children decided they had to go back to the ranch and talk to Aunt Jane.

Let's not worry. Things always work out all right for us.

Aunt Jane! You're up and dressed! I was never so glad in my life!

Tell me everything that happened.

The children told her everything. The told her about Mr. Carter, and how he and the Sheriff caught the three bad men. And they told her that the land was rich with minerals.

Mr. Carter says we must have help from some man who can do things in a big way and who has money to build a mine.

But I wonder if he would after the way I've treated him. I could never manage the hundreds of people running all over my ranch-- I mean your ranch.

I'm sure Grandfather would help.

Aunt Jane decided to write a letter and ask her brother for his help. Everyone was so excited that they could hardly contain themselves.

I know one man who can do it. My brother, James Alden--your grandfather.

THE BOSS

Things moved quickly. Grandfather made sure everything ran smoothly. A mine was dug. Big machines worked day and night. Houses for workmen were built.

To make sure Aunt Jane wasn't disturbed by the miners, a fence was built around the ranch's property.

Aunt Jane, why didn't you let your own brother help you when you needed money?

When my father and mother went East, your Grandfather wanted to sell the ranch. But I decided to stay here. I wouldn't give in and admit I needed help. I was stubborn.

Aunt Jane decided to throw a party. Everyone helped out to make sure it was the best party ever.

Grandfather!

Brother! You're here! Can you ever forgive me for how horribly I behaved?

There's nothing to forgive!

Mr. Carter was also invited to the party. Everyone had a wonderful time.

After dinner, Aunt Jane opened her presents.

I love every one of my presents.

Grandfather has a present, too.

Her name is Lady. To take the place of Watch when the children go home.

The rest of the summer was spent together as a happy family. Everyone thought it was the best summer any of them could remember.

ABOUT THE CREATOR

Gertrude Chandler Warner was born on April 16, 1890, in Putnam, Connecticut. In 1918, Warner began teaching at Israel Putnam School. As a teacher, she discovered that many readers who liked an exciting story could not find books that were both easy and fun to read. She decided to try to meet this need. In 1942, *The Boxcar Children* was published for these readers.

Warner drew on her own experience to write *The Boxcar Children*. As a child she spent hours watching trains go by on the tracks near her family home. She often dreamed about what it would be like to live in a caboose or freight car—just as the Alden children do.

When readers asked for more Alden adventures, Warner began additional stories. While the mystery element is central to each of the books, she never thought of them as strictly juvenile mysteries. She liked to stress the Aldens' independence. Henry, Jessie, Violet, and Benny go about most of their adventures with as little adult supervision as possible—something that delights young readers.

During her lifetime, Warner received hundreds of letters from fans as she continued the Aldens' adventures, writing nineteen Boxcar Children books in all. After her death in 1979, her publisher, Albert Whitman and Company, carried on Warner's vision. Today, the Boxcar Children series has more than 100 books.